HOW TO WRITE A BOOK IN A WEEK

by
David Dowson

www.daviddowson.com
daviddowson4@gmail.com

Acknowledgements

Special thanks to my mother, Beryl, who is always there for me and my sister, Jan Webber, Author of the *Betty Illustrated* Children's books.

Other books also written by David Dowson include:

Chess for Beginners
Chess for Beginners Edition 2
Into the Realm of Chess Calculation
Nursery Rhymes
The Path of a Chess Amateur

BEGINNERS GUIDE eBook:
- Declon Five.
- Dangers within
- The murder of Inspector Hine
- Spooks

- Uranium 235

-

CHAPTER ONE

- Introduction
  Writing a book is a goal for every writer. If you're reading this book, it is one of your strongest desires. But I know that writing a book is easier said than done. You cannot open your laptop and start writing.

- You've been delaying it for months, even years, or lack the confidence to complete the work. But what if I said you could finish your book in a week while keeping the quality you anticipated? Yes, it is possible. All you need is seven days, a solid plan, and lots of confidence. However, refraining from DISTRACTING ACTIVITIES for the next seven days would be best. Also, do not take up any new projects like decorating the house until you finish this writing project. It might seem a bit absurd and challenging to Write a book in a week, especially if you are new to writing, but it is possible. So, as a brief overview, here's what your next seven days will look like.

Something like this:

- Day 1: Make a plan (self-assessment, brainstorming ideas, and calculating your word count).

- Day 2: Research and outline chapters. We will look at **outlining your book** later.

- Day 3, 4, 5, 6: Begin writing(you will not sleep much)

- Day 7: Finish writing and editing
  You can get editing and Proofreading done at *www.Fiverr.co.uk* *(I would appreciate if you mention my name when you join).*

Embarking on the journey of writing a book is a dream in every aspiring Author's heart. If you read these lines, the desire to see your thoughts and stories come to life on paper has become a burning passion. Yet, we understand the challenges that often accompany such aspirations. Writing a book is more than just a declaration; it requires dedication, motivation, and a strategic approach.

Unfortunately, sitting down and effortlessly pouring your ideas onto a blank page is a romanticised version of the writing process.
Completing a book in a week is an ambitious goal, and while it might be possible for some writers, it's essential to approach it with a

realistic mindset. Quality writing typically requires time, effort, and careful consideration. However, if you're up for a challenge and are willing to make some sacrifices, here are a few tips that might help you expedite the writing process:

1. **Set Clear Goals:** Define each day's word count or chapter target. This can help you stay focused and on track to meet your deadline.

2. **Eliminate Distractions:** Create a dedicated writing space free from distractions. Turn off social media, email notifications, and other potential

interruptions to maintain focus during your writing sessions.

3. **Time Management:** Allocate specific time blocks for writing and stick to them. Whether it's early in the morning, late at night, or during lunch breaks, having a consistent schedule can help you make steady progress.

4. **Minimise Editing:** Resist the urge to edit as you write. Instead, focus on getting your ideas down on paper. You can always go back and refine your work during the editing phase.

5. **Stay Inspired:** Keep your motivation high by reminding

yourself of the reasons you're writing this book. Whether it's a personal goal, a message you want to share, or a story you're passionate about, staying connected to your inspiration can help you push through challenges.

6. **Use Writing Prompts:** If you find yourself stuck, consider using writing prompts to jumpstart your creativity. This can help you overcome moments of self-doubt and keep the ideas flowing.

7. **Limit Research:** If your book requires research, limit the time spent during the initial drafting

phase. You can go back and fill in the details during the editing process.

8. **Stay Healthy:** Taking care of your physical and mental well-being is crucial. Ensure you sleep well, stay hydrated, and take short breaks to recharge your mind.

9. **Have a Plan:** Outline your book before you start writing. A clear roadmap can prevent you from getting stuck and help you move swiftly through your narrative.

10. **Accountability:** Share your goal with someone who can hold you accountable.

Whether it's a friend, family member, or writing partner, having someone check your progress can motivate you.

While speed can be an asset, quality should not be compromised. If you find that the quality of your writing is suffering, it might be worth considering a more realistic timeline or focusing on specific sections of your book first.

Have you envisioned quality? Yes, you read that right. All it takes is seven days, a well-crafted plan, and a dash of confidence.

Of course, this endeavour comes with sacrifices. For the next seven days, you'll need to put aside social engagements and resist the temptation of new projects. It may seem unconventional and, at times, challenging, especially for those new to the writing scene, but rest assured, it is entirely feasible. In this guide, we'll walk you through a streamlined process that will help you transform your book from an idea to a tangible manuscript.

Let's take another glance at the *seven-day plan* in more detail and at what the next stage of the *seven days* will look like:

Day 1: Make a Plan

- Engage in self-assessment and brainstorming to crystallise your ideas.

- Divide your word count to create a manageable writing schedule.

Day 2: Outline Chapters

- Dive into necessary research to enhance the depth and authenticity of your narrative.

- Create a detailed outline to serve as your roadmap during the writing process.

Days 3, 4, 5, and 6 Begin your Writing

- Channel your energy into translating your thoughts into words.

- Stick to the plan and let the creativity flow as you draft your chapters.

Day 7: Wrapping Up and Editing

- Wrap up any remaining sections of your book.

- Dedicate time to editing and refining your manuscript for quality and coherence.

This guide aims to be your companion throughout this intensive journey. By these seven days, you'll have a completed manuscript and a newfound confidence to realise your writing dreams. So, let's dive in and make your authorial aspirations a swift and successful endeavour.

CHAPTER TWO

Setting Realistic Goals

Setting realistic goals based on the number of days available is crucial in the initial phase of your writing journey. Assess your daily schedule, commitments, and energy levels. Determine a reasonable word count target for each writing session, considering your personal writing speed and the complexity of your content. This chapter will guide you through establishing achievable milestones that keep you on track without compromising quality.

- Planning and Outlining

Before diving into the writing process, invest time in comprehensive planning and outlining. Develop a solid structure for your book, outlining key plot points, themes, and character arcs. This chapter will help you create a roadmap for your writing journey, making navigating easier and preventing writer's block. A well-thought-out plan enhances the coherence of your narrative and minimises the risk of going off track.

- Daily Writing Rituals

Establishing a consistent writing routine is essential for progress. I hope to provide practical advice on creating daily rituals that boost creativity and focus. From choosing an optimal writing environment to managing distractions, you'll learn how to maximise your writing time. Developing habits that align with your goals will contribute to a steady and sustainable writing pace.

- Overcoming Writer's Block

Even the most seasoned writers encounter periods of stagnation. I offer strategies to overcome writer's block, providing tips on reigniting creativity and finding inspiration. Whether through changing your writing environment, seeking feedback, or experimenting with different writing exercises, you'll learn how to navigate obstacles and keep the creative momentum flowing.

- Quality vs. Quantity

Maintaining a balance between quantity and quality is paramount. I explores strategies for producing content efficiently without sacrificing the integrity of your work. Learn to recognise when to push forward and when to revisit and refine your writing. Striking this balance ensures you meet your deadlines while delivering a polished and impactful manuscript.

- Editing and Revisions

Once the initial draft is complete, the focus shifts to editing and revisions. I guide you through self-editing, offering tips on enhancing clarity, tightening prose, and refining your narrative. Understanding the importance of multiple drafts and seeking external feedback will contribute to a final manuscript that meets your vision and resonates with your audience.

- It's a Wrap.

Quick Note

You must go over and over the program of this book .

I hope you will finish your story as you approach the final days of your writing journey. From completing the last chapters to celebrating your achievements, you'll learn to conclude your writing project gracefully. Embrace the sense of accomplishment and prepare for the next steps in bringing your dream project to fruition.

By following this guide, you'll navigate the writing process effectively, ensuring that your book meets your deadlines and reflects the depth and quality you envision for your dream project.

CHAPTER THREE

Below is a list of ideas you may want to go over.

Day 1 - Making a Plan

Welcome to the first day of your exciting writing journey! Today is all about laying the groundwork for your project. Let's break down the essential tasks to ensure a strong foundation for your book.

1. **Personal Assessment:**
   - Reflect on your strengths and weaknesses as a writer.

- Identify your peak productivity hours and allocate dedicated writing time accordingly.

- Consider any potential distractions and develop strategies to minimise them.

2. **Brainstorming Main Subject:**

- Dive deep into the core theme or subject of your book.

- Jot down key ideas, articles, or messages you want to convey.

- Consider the target audience and how your

book will resonate with
them.

3. **Word Count Allocation:**

- Determine the overall
  word count goal for your
  book.

- Break down the word
  count into manageable
  daily targets based on the
  total days you have for the
  project.

- Establish a realistic and
  achievable daily writing
  goal.

4. **Create a Project Timeline:**

- Develop a timeline that outlines milestones and deadlines.

- Set specific dates for completing each chapter or section.

- Include regular review points to assess your progress and make any necessary adjustments to your plan.

5. **Set Up Your Writing Space:**

- Arrange a comfortable and inspiring writing environment.

- Gather necessary writing tools and materials.

- Minimise potential distractions in your workspace.

6. **Motivational Boost:**

- Remind yourself of the significance of your project.

- Set personal and project-related goals to stay motivated throughout the journey.

- Visualise the sense of accomplishment upon completing your book.

7. **Prepare for Tomorrow:**

- Outline the tasks you'll tackle on Day 2.

- Review your plan and make any adjustments if needed.

- Ensure you have all the resources and information required for the next steps.

Congratulations on completing Day 1! Your plan is now in place, providing a solid foundation for the days ahead. You can dive into the writing process with a clear roadmap and turn your ideas into a compelling narrative. Tomorrow, you'll begin shaping your story and bringing it to life. Get ready for an exciting journey ahead!

Chapter FOUR

Planning and Outlining

Before diving into the writing process, invest time in comprehensive planning and outlining. Develop a solid foundation for your book, like a building. Without a solid foundation, it will crumble. Outline key plot points, themes, and character arcs. I try to help you create a roadmap for your writing journey, making navigating easier and preventing writer's block. A well-thought-out plan enhances the coherence of your narrative and minimises the risk of going off track.

3: Daily Writing Rituals

Establishing a consistent writing routine is essential for progress. This chapter provides practical advice on creating daily rituals that boost creativity and focus. From choosing an optimal writing environment to managing distractions, you'll learn how to maximise your writing time. Developing habits that align with your goals will contribute to a steady and sustainable writing pace.

5: Quality vs. Quantity

Maintaining a balance between quantity and quality is paramount. This chapter explores strategies for producing content efficiently without sacrificing the integrity of your work. Learn to recognise when to push forward and when to revisit and refine your writing. Striking this balance ensures you meet your deadlines while delivering a polished and impactful manuscript.

Editing and Revisions

Once the initial draft is complete, the focus shifts to editing and revisions. This chapter guides you through self-editing, offering tips on enhancing clarity, tightening prose, and refining your narrative. Understanding the importance of multiple drafts and seeking external feedback will contribute to a final manuscript that meets your vision and resonates with your audience.

Wrapping It Up

As you approach the final days of your writing journey, this chapter guides you in finishing strong. From completing the last chapters to celebrating your achievements, you'll learn to conclude your writing project gracefully. Embrace the sense of accomplishment and prepare for the next steps in bringing your dream project to fruition.

By following this guide, you'll navigate the writing process effectively, ensuring that your book meets your deadlines and reflects the depth and quality you envision for your dream project.

Into the project is crucial as it will form the basis for your book. The foundation should be robust in any project. One will take the first day to formulate your plan, keeping things in order and helping you finish your project quickly. The first day will involve completing essential but necessary tasks to begin writing your book. This will include conducting a personal assessment test, brainstorming ideas for your main subject, and dividing your word count for the rest of the days of the project. This will give you a definite head start on this project and motivate you to begin working on it.

CHAPTER FIVE

Recap

• **Day 1 - Make a Plan Your first day** into the project is crucial as it will form the basis for your book. The foundation should be robust in any project. You will take the first day to formulate your plan. Which will keep things in order and help you finish your project quickly. The first day will involve completing essential but necessary tasks to begin writing your book.

This includes conducting a personal assessment test, brainstorming ideas for your main subject, and dividing your word count for the rest of the project days. Which will give you a definite head start on this project and motivate you to begin working on it.

Making a Plan

Welcome to the first day of your exciting writing journey! Today is all about laying the groundwork for your project. Let's break down the essential tasks to ensure a strong foundation for your book.

1. **Personal Assessment:**

- Reflect on your strengths and weaknesses as a writer.

- Identify your peak productivity hours and allocate dedicated writing time accordingly.

- Consider any potential distractions and develop strategies to minimise them.

2. Brainstorming Main Subject:

- Dive deep into the core theme or subject of your book.

- Jot down key ideas, articles, or messages you want to convey.

- Consider the target audience and how your book will resonate with them.

3. **Word Count Allocation:**

- Determine the overall word count goal for your book.

- Break down the word count into manageable daily targets based on the total days you have for the project.

- Establish a realistic and achievable daily writing goal.

4. Create a Project Timeline:

- Develop a timeline that outlines milestones and deadlines.

- Set specific dates for completing each chapter or section.

- Include regular review points to assess your progress and make any necessary adjustments to your plan.

5. Set Up Your Writing Space:

- Arrange a comfortable and inspiring writing environment.

- Gather necessary writing tools and materials.

- Minimise potential distractions in your workspace.

6. **Motivational Boost:**

- Remind yourself of the significance of your project.

- Set personal and project-related goals to stay motivated throughout the journey.

- Visualise the sense of accomplishment upon completing your book.

7. **Prepare for Tomorrow:**

Outline the tasks you'll tackle on Day 2.

Review your plan and make any adjustments if needed.

Ensure you have all the resources and information required for the next steps.

Well done if you have got this far on completing! A book.

Your plan is now in place, providing a solid foundation for the days ahead. You can dive into the writing process with a clear roadmap and turn your ideas into a compelling narrative. Tomorrow, you'll begin shaping your story and bringing it to life. Get ready for an exciting journey ahead!

Embarking on the journey of writing a book is not just about the 'what' and 'how,' but, more importantly, the 'why.' Taking the time for self-assessment will provide valuable insights into your motivations, aspirations, and the purpose behind your writing endeavour.

Ask yourself why you want to write this book.

Consider whether you aim to share a personal story, convey a powerful message, or contribute to a specific field. Reflect on how this project aligns with your long-term goals and aspirations.

Clarify the central message or theme you want to convey through your book.

Articulate the key ideas or lessons you hope readers will take away from your work.

Explore how your unique perspective can make a meaningful impact.

1. **Authorial Identity:**

   - Envision how you want to be perceived as an author.

   - Consider the tone, style, and voice you want to convey in your writing.

- Reflect on what sets your authorial identity apart and makes it compelling to your target audience.

2. **Motivational Factors:**

- Pinpoint the aspects of writing that truly motivate and inspire you.

- Identify potential challenges and how overcoming them contributes to your personal growth.

- Recognise how achieving your writing goals aligns with your overall sense of fulfilment.

-

3. Brand Growth and Marketing:

- Assess whether your book is a strategic move for brand growth and marketing.

- Explore how the book aligns with your brand's values and mission.

- Consider the target audience and how the book contributes to building a connection with them.

-

- **Mission Statement:**

"To inspire and empower readers by weaving narratives exploring the depths of human experience, challenging perspectives, and igniting a sense of curiosity. Through storytelling, I aim to foster connection, provoke thought, and leave a lasting impact that resonates with the hearts and minds of my audience. My 'why' is to create a space for reflection, growth, and understanding, sparking conversations that transcend the pages of my book and contribute to a more enriched and compassionate world."

This mission statement encapsulates the core purpose behind the writing journey: to inspire, empower, and create a meaningful connection with the audience. It will be a constant reminder of the overarching goal and guide the writing process, ensuring that each word contributes to fulfilling this mission.

Devising Ideas: Finding the Heart of Your Story

If you find yourself at a crossroads without a specific book idea, don't worry—this brainstorming exercise will help you discover your book's compelling plot or subject. Whether you're aiming for fiction or non-fiction, follow these steps to unearth the heart of your story:

Explore Your Interests:

List your hobbies, passions, and areas of expertise. Consider topics that genuinely excite and engage you. Think about what you enjoy discussing or learning about in your free time.

Identify Personal Experiences:

Reflect on significant moments or experiences in your life. Consider challenges you've overcome or lessons you've learned. Your unique perspective can add authenticity and depth to your writing.

Current Trends and Issues:

Stay informed about current events and societal trends. Explore issues that resonate with you or that you believe need more attention. Consider how your perspective can contribute to the ongoing conversation.

Character Exploration:

If you're leaning towards fiction, brainstorm exciting characters.

Consider their backgrounds, motivations, and conflicts they might face.

Characters can often drive the plot and make it more engaging for readers.

Genre Consideration:

Consider the genre you want to write in (e.g., mystery, romance, science fiction, self-help).

- Consider the conventions and themes associated with that genre.

- Brainstorm ideas that align with or subvert these conventions.

What-If Scenarios:

Play with "what-if" scenarios to spark creativity. Consider unusual or unexpected situations and imagine their outcomes. This can lead to unique and captivating storylines.

Combine Ideas:

Mix and match different elements from your brainstorming. Combining interests, experiences, or scenarios creates a rich and multifaceted narrative. Sometimes, the most intriguing ideas emerge from unexpected combinations.

Research and Inspiration:

Delve into books, articles, or artworks that inspire you. Look for gaps or areas where you can contribute a fresh perspective. Research can provide valuable insights and ignite new ideas.

Feedback Loop:

Share your initial ideas with friends, family, or writing groups. Gather feedback and insights to refine and strengthen your concept. External perspectives can offer valuable perspectives and help you see potential blind spots. Remember, the goal is not to settle on the perfect idea immediately but to explore and refine it until you find a concept that resonates with you. Allow yourself the freedom to be creative and open-minded during this process. Once you've identified a promising idea, you can begin shaping it into the foundation of your book.

Make a list of things that you are good at. Whether it's cooking, painting, or playing sports, list the tasks that you can master. It is not confined to your talents; you can also jot down your skills as your former or current profession - a stockbroker, teacher, or therapist. This will help you choose a topic for your non-fiction book unless you have already decided. While at it, choose a topic or subject you can quickly write about without conducting thorough research. This is why we list the issues you have experience or expertise in. It would be best also to contemplate the questions your friends or close acquaintances often ask you about. Do they often come to you for relationship advice? Or do they ask you about real estate? Reflect on the subjects, and you will be able to come up with a concrete topic to write about.

NOVEL WORD COUNT CALCULATING your Word Count

A fiction novel usually has a word count ranging from 45,000 words upwards.

They are delivering the message. Readers, especially those trying to get back into reading, prefer short reads as they are easier to finish. So, you are good to go. You can also increase your word count if your story demands.

The truth is, an intelligent man does not read more pages than others. He reads ten pages and obtains the same amount of information instead of reading 100 pages of repetitive data. He saves time and gains knowledge simultaneously. So, don't worry about your word count. Stick to what your subject demands, whether a short or long book. Hence, the length of your book should be the least of your concerns. It is only necessary to fix the size and final word count to Divide your time accordingly and get the work done on time.

1: Calculate Your Word Count

In this chapter, we tackle the crucial task of determining the optimal word count for your fiction novel. Recognise the average range for fiction works from 45,000 to over

50,000 words. However, we'll also explore the rising preference for shorter reads, considering the ease with which readers can complete them. Learn why your story's demands should guide your word count decisions rather than conforming to a predetermined standard.

2: Quality Over Quantity

Delve into the mindset of an intelligent reader. It's not about consuming more pages but extracting maximum value from each word. Discover the art of conveying a powerful message without unnecessary repetition. Uncover the secrets to condensing information, saving time, and enhancing reader engagement. Understand why your focus should be on the substance of your narrative, not the sheer volume of words.

3: Tailoring Your Word Count to Your Story

Explore the freedom of adjusting your word count based on your narrative's needs. Find the balance that suits your message, whether your story demands brevity or expansiveness. This chapter emphasises that the length of your book should not be a source of stress but rather a tool to structure your writing journey effectively.

4: Setting Realistic Goals

Learn to set practical and achievable word count goals to divide your writing time effectively. Understand the importance of aligning your goals with the needs of your narrative. This chapter provides a roadmap for staying on track, avoiding unnecessary pressure, and ensuring the completion of your novel within the designated timeframe.

Conclusion: Word Counts as Guiding Lights

As you conclude this chapter, appreciate that your word count is not a rigid constraint but a guiding light. Let the demands of your story dictate the length, and use it as a tool to manage your time efficiently. It would be best to focus on delivering a compelling narrative rather than fixating on arbitrary word count standards. So, read on, embrace the flexibility of word counts, and pave the way for a successful and stress-free writing journey. The initial planning phase is a critical foundation for the entire book-writing process. This phase sets the tone, structure, and direction for your work. Here are some key aspects to consider during the planning phase.

- **Setting the Stage (Day 1)**

Delve into the crucial first day of your writing journey. Learn how to conduct a <u>self-assessment</u>, harness your creative ideas, and strategically calculate your daily word count.

Building the Framework (Day 2)

Discover the significance of thorough research and compelling chapter outlining. Day 2 is all about creating a roadmap for your book. We'll guide you through gathering information that adds depth to your narrative and structuring your chapters for a seamless writing experience.

- **Putting Pen to Paper (Days 3, 4, 5)**

The heart of your writing endeavour unfolds in these three chapters. Dive into the writing process with tips on maintaining quality while meeting your daily word count goals. Overcome writer's block, tap into your creativity, and witness your manuscript taking shape.

- **The Final Stretch (Day 6)**

As your writing journey nears its end, this chapter guides you in wrapping up your book. We'll explore strategies for finishing the remaining sections and dedicate time to the crucial task of editing. Learn how to refine your work, ensuring your message is clear and your prose is polished.

- **Celebrating Your Success**

This concluding section is not just the end of your SEVEN-day writing sprint; it's the beginning of your life as a published

author. Reflect on your accomplishments, acknowledge your dedication to your work, and embrace the newfound confidence in your writing abilities.

As you read through these chapters, remember that commitment and a well-structured plan are the keys to success. By following this guide, you're not just writing a book but achieving a dream. So, read on, absorb the advice, and let's turn your aspirations into a tangible reality. Your dream project is within reach, and these pages will guide you to making it happen.

Crafting a Realistic Writing Schedule

In this chapter, we address the practicalities of writing a substantial number of words in a limited time frame. Acknowledge the challenges of writing 25,000 words in just a few days, especially for those who may not have extensive experience in novel writing. Discover that the key to success lies in a well-thought-out plan.

Strategic Division of Writing Days

Learn the art of calculating your total word count across the available days.

Internalise that successful writing isn't just about speed; it's about strategic planning. By intelligently dividing your word count and setting achievable targets, you maximise your chances of completing your book within the specified timeframe. So, read on, absorb the advice, and let's turn your ambitious word count into an achievable reality.

Understand that, as a writer, your initial days are not solely dedicated to writing but include crucial tasks like assessment, research, chapter outlines, and even deciding on a title. Delve into the specifics of allocating time for editing on the final day, leaving you with a condensed period for actual writing.

Setting Achievable Daily Targets

Establish practical daily word count targets to make the daunting task more manageable. Depending on your available writing days, calculate the number of words you need to write each day to meet your overall goal. Whether it's 7500 or 8000 words per day, this chapter guides you in setting realistic targets considering your writing speed and the time required for effective editing.

Adapting to Your Writing Speed

Explore the impact of your typing speed on your writing goals. Assess the time it takes to produce a certain number of words and tailor your daily targets accordingly. Whether you're a fast typist or just starting, this chapter provides insights into adjusting your goals to match your capabilities.

Flexibility in Execution

Understand that plans may need to be adjusted. If you efficiently complete your research and outlining on day 2, consider starting the writing process earlier. This chapter emphasises the importance of adapting to your progress and making the most of your writing days.

Writing Smart, Not Just Fast

Before you conclude this section,

Here are some essential pointers. Ensure your words convey a motivational and encouraging tone, which can be powerful for someone embarking on writing a book. Turning aspirations into a tangible reality requires dedication, perseverance, and a strategic approach. Here are a few additional tips to complement the guidance you've read.

1. **Cultivate a Positive Mindset:** Approach the writing process

with a positive mindset. Believe in your ability to bring your ideas to life and overcome challenges.

2. **Celebrate Small Wins:** Acknowledge and celebrate small achievements as you progress through your writing journey. It could be reaching a word count goal, completing a challenging chapter, or receiving positive feedback.

3. **Stay Flexible:** While having a plan is essential, be open to adapting it as needed. Sometimes, the creative process takes unexpected turns, and being flexible allows for

organic and authentic storytelling.

4. **Seek Support:** Share your writing journey with friends, family, or fellow writers. A support system can encourage you during moments of self-doubt and keep you accountable.

5. **Visualise Success:** Envision the successful completion of your book. Visualising the result can motivate and help you focus on your ultimate goal.

6. **Take Breaks:** It's essential to recharge your creativity. Short breaks can help you return to writing with a fresh perspective

if you feel stuck or overwhelmed.

7. **Embrace Imperfection:** Understand that perfection is often an unattainable goal. Embrace the imperfections in your first draft, knowing that the editing process is where your work will truly shine.

8. **Connect with Your Passion:** Reconnect with the passion that drove you to start this project. Whether it's a love for storytelling, a desire to share knowledge, or a personal journey, staying connected to your passion fuels the writing process.

9. **Reflect and Adjust:**
Periodically reflect on your progress and adjust your approach if necessary. Learning from your experiences can enhance your writing skills and improve your overall process.

10. **Celebrate the Completion:** When you reach the end of your writing journey, take the time to celebrate the completion of your book. It's a significant accomplishment; recognising your achievement is essential for your fulfilment.

Remember, every writer's journey is unique, and there's no one-size-fits-all approach. By combining practical advice with a positive mindset and perseverance, aspiring authors can transform their dreams into a tangible reality.

Printed in Great Britain
by Amazon